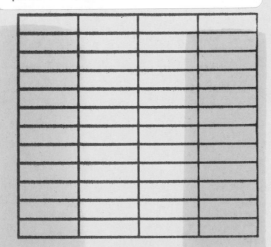

The
Barefoot Book of
MOTHER
—— AND ——
SON
TALES

For my son Ben, whose gift was moccasins
— J. E.-S.
For my mother — H.C.

Barefoot Collections

an imprint of

Barefoot Books

41 Schermerhorn Street,

Suite 145, Brooklyn,

New York

NY 11201-4845

Library of Congress Cataloging-in-Publication Data is available on request.

ISBN 1 902283 05 8

Graphic design by Design/Section, Frome

Color separation by Grafiscan, Verona

This book has been printed on 100% acid-free paper

Printed in Hong Kong by South Sea International Press

1 3 5 7 9 8 6 4 2

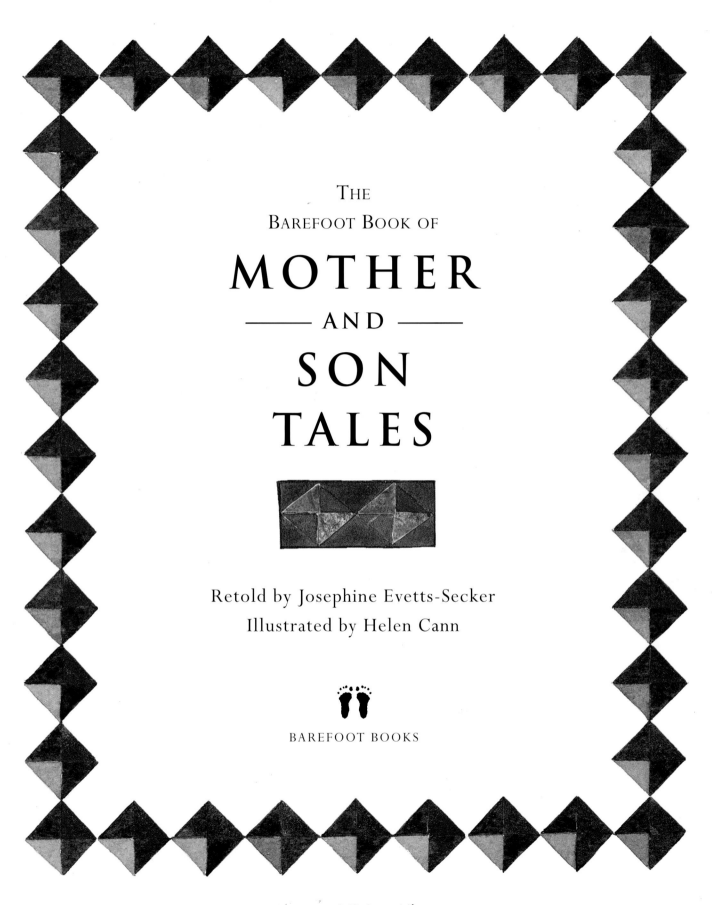

THE
BAREFOOT BOOK OF
MOTHER
— AND —
SON
TALES

Retold by Josephine Evetts-Secker
Illustrated by Helen Cann

BAREFOOT BOOKS

CONTENTS

FOREWORD

These tales from around the world deal in one way or another with what has been called "the secret conspiracy" between mother and son, a bond that can be life-enhancing or destructive. Either way, whatever is established early on will abide throughout life unless some change is brought about by the son.

The mother's great secret is, of course, her power over life and her access to the abundance of nature. Her essential mystery is that she is both the source of life, yet simultaneously, as Mother Earth, she is the final rest towards which life moves. Without her energy and provision, her sons will go hungry and live apart from nature; life cannot be sustained without her. Yet the personal mother is to be left behind. Her sons must leave her in order to embrace the world of the father and eventually to claim another partner. So this primary relationship must end – primary in intensity and primary because it is the first and originating bond, a biological union that can never be replicated. The son's ultimate goal is to become a man and most often to become a father. Unless he matures, he will end up as son rather than husband to his bride and he will not be able to be father to his son, though this latter stage is left implicit in folk and fairy tales, which usually end with marriage.

This collection of tales ranges from North America to Nepal. Everywhere mothers are seen to be protective and caring, though such protection and care are also shown to have a negative aspect. The Selkup mother in "The Mistress of Fire" is so angry when her child is burned that she responds with an aggression that has terrible cosmic consequences. The world is a dangerous place and sons must be allowed to live life fully amidst its perils, though mothers would like to keep them safe at home. The pull is always towards separation, though the call home, to mother (the two are often identical), is always active. This tension is essential. When a mother would keep her son to herself and in safety, there will be a healthy contradictory impulse to leave; but when the son wants to stay in the comfortable embrace of his mother, she will push him out of the nest … or consume him. Only when the son's task is fulfilled, his apprenticeship in the father's world served, may he return home, his treasure won. All of these possibilities are enacted in these stories, though most commonly it is the outward journey that excites the storyteller.

The sons in these tales are both exceptional and ordinary – one is even an ugly impostor ("The Changeling of Llanfabon"); but the dynamics of development are the same whatever their situation or talents. Some are brave, avid for adventure and curious about the mysteries of life, pursuing the gods themselves to answer their questions, such as the boy in "The Goddess of Luck." Some are reluctant to leave the mother and have to be bribed, as in the case of Cinderello. Many are only sons, but some have siblings whom they love and by whom they are loved and/or hated, as in "Snot-Nose" and "The Magical Sweetgrass Doll." Envy between brothers is a common motif.

Like the sons, the mothers in this collection vary enormously in character and temperament. Good mothers rub shoulders with ogresses, bold midwives and sisters with giantesses, poor widows with goddesses, would-be brides with faerie folk, princesses and queens with beggar-women. Many of the mothers live alone with their sons, which puts even greater pressure on the mother–son bond. Such lonely mothers show courage in rearing their sons with few outer resources, though this poverty can be a trap to detain the son at home, as it is in "The Goddess of Luck." Perhaps the most inspiring and poignant model for a healthy mother–son relationship is that of the Wabanaki mother ("The Magical Sweetgrass Doll"), who lovingly sews for her son's journey the very moccasins that will carry him away from her.

Josephine Evetts-Secker

THE GODDESS OF LUCK

NEPALESE

In a lonely village high in the mountains of Nepal there once lived an old woman who had one son. They were very poor and could only survive by doing the meanest of jobs for other people. When things were very bad, they even had to beg. As he grew older, the boy became more and more discontented with this life. One day he asked, "Mother, why are we so poor? Why do we have so little to eat or wear?"

His mother said quietly, "We must accept it, my son, for it is the will of the gods. It is our fate."

But the boy was not at all satisfied with this answer and he decided to set off at once to find the Lord of the Universe, to ask the same question. Of course, he was hoping for a better answer. After many hours, he reached a thick jungle. By now, he was exhausted and hungry, so he sat down to rest.

By chance, the god and goddess Siva and Parvati were passing by. When Siva saw the boy, he asked, "O little one, what are you doing all by yourself in this frightening place?"

The boy told Siva and Parvati about his mother who was so poor that she had to beg. "I am going to find the Lord of the Universe to ask him why we are so poor. Once I have learned the answer, I will become rich."

The god and goddess were touched by the boy's story and Parvati said to Siva, "My lord, we must give something to this child, at once."

Siva shook his head slowly. "No, my dear Parvati, this we cannot do. For the boy and his mother must receive only what Fate has decreed for them. Anything else they gain will soon be lost and they will be worse off than before."

Parvati was not satisfied with this. She pestered Siva until at last he changed his mind and offered to give the boy a gold necklace. The boy was delighted! He took the necklace with smiles and thanks and set off home to his mother. But as he walked, he grew sicker and sicker. When he could bear it no longer, he put down his pack and his necklace so that he could go into the bushes to relieve himself. While he did so, a great eagle flew by. Seeing the sparkle of gold, it swooped down and flew off with the necklace.

The poor boy wept all the way home. What was worse, when he finally got back, his mother would not believe a word he said. "What a farfetched tale," she snorted. "Now you get down to the village and find some useful work so that you can earn some bread."

But the next day, the boy decided that he must set out again to find the Lord of the Universe and to ask him why they were so poor. He crept out of the house before his mother woke up, and he walked and walked till his body ached. At last, he came to the same spot as the day before. Once again, Siva and Parvati were passing by. Again, they stopped to talk with him and asked, "How did you fare with the gold necklace we gave you?" They were sad to hear how he had lost it, but Siva insisted that until the boy's luck changed, he would not be able to keep anything he might be given.

Parvati again felt great pity for the boy and begged Siva to help him. When her husband said that he could do nothing, she persuaded him to go with her to the great Lord Brahma in his home high above the mountains and to ask him for help. So away they went. "This boy has much courage, great Lord; please do something to help such a special child," the couple begged. The great Lord Brahma listened carefully to their story. Then he offered Parvati a diamond ring to take back to the boy.

With the ring in his pocket and joy in his heart the boy took to the road again. Of course he grew thirsty and after a while he stopped by a stream for a drink. But as he knelt down to scoop up some water, the ring fell out of his pocket and was immediately devoured by a fish. The poor boy could barely believe his eyes! He cried and cried as he ran home, but his mother said, "You foolish child! How can you expect me to believe such a tale?"

Night came and went, and by morning the boy felt strong again and was more determined than ever to have an answer to his question. He walked till mid-afternoon and then sat down to rest. Once more, Siva and Parvati came by. The first thing they wanted to know was whether he had managed to take his treasure back to his mother.

"Oh no," the boy said and he wept. "I ran till I could run no more without drinking some water. When I knelt down to drink from the stream, the ring

fell into the water and was devoured by a fish. But still I must find the Lord of the Universe to know the answer to my question."

Now Siva was touched by the boy's tears, so he decided to visit the great Lord Brahma again. Between them, Brahma and Siva agreed to approach Vishnu himself to gain something for the child. When he heard the boy's story, even Vishnu was moved. So he decided to give the boy some diamonds.

This time, the boy hurried straight home, not wanting to lose his treasure on the journey again. He ran and ran without stopping to drink and reached their hut before his mother had returned from her begging. So he put the diamonds in a safe place and went in search of her, calling to her loudly in his excitement.

Hardly daring to believe his story, his mother hurried back to the hut, only to find that a thief had broken in and stolen everything! Now she was really angry and she scolded her son for spending his days running off and making up stories, when he should be out begging or looking for work. The poor boy went quietly out into the fields and sobbed in disappointment.

But by the next morning he was feeling better again, and he set off once more for the jungle. Siva could scarcely believe that despite all his troubles and losses, the boy had not given up. "How amazing is this boy's spirit," he said to Parvati. This time, he went straight to the Goddess of Luck to ask her to do something to help the child.

The Goddess of Luck was so impressed that she came down to the jungle herself and gave the boy one copper coin. Although it was just one coin, the boy thanked her politely and bounded off to take his treasure home. He ran to his mother and hugged her, saying, "Now I have some wealth, mother, and

we need no longer go begging." They laughed together and took great care of his coin.

Soon after this, a fisherman came by selling his catch. This time they could buy something. "Please give us a big fish," the boy said contentedly, "for today we have money to buy one."

Then the boy took a knife to prepare the fish for the fire. Imagine his astonishment when he cut it open! For there in the fish's gut was the ring that had fallen into the stream. "How lucky we are, mother!" he cried out in delight. And his mother took the ring and looked at it in amazement.

Then the boy climbed a tree nearby, looking for some wood to stoke the fire. Right at the top of the tree was an eagle's nest. When the boy looked inside it, he was even more amazed to find the gold necklace that he had lost! But that was only the second bit of luck. When he came down from the tree, he found the thief at the door of the hut. The night after he had robbed them, the thief had had a dream which told him that he must give the diamonds back to the poor folk he had stolen them from.

This is how the Goddess of Luck helped a poor mother and her son to become rich!

THE MAGICAL
SWEETGRASS DOLL

WABANAKI

Kayak was a Wabanaki boy who lived long ago in the Old Time. He was the youngest and cleverest of seven sons: he could shoot straight with his arrows and he could swim, run and fight better than all his older brothers. He thought about things and worked hard at everything he attempted. So of course his brothers grew jealous of him and they always tried to get him into trouble by telling lies about him to his parents and the elders.

Kayak was so troubled by this that when he was twelve years old, he decided to run away from home. Day after day, he trained himself carefully. He wanted to make sure that he could run faster than his brothers, so that if they tried to follow him they wouldn't be able to catch him. He practiced by shooting an arrow into the air and racing to reach it before it hit the target. He did this over and over again, shooting further each time so that he would have to run harder and harder. Soon he could run faster than the deer!

Now, Kayak's mother loved him dearly. She knew that he was unhappy and that he wanted to leave home. So while he was practicing, she sewed new moccasins to protect his feet on his journey. She chose the softest doeskin and she made every stitch with love and care. When the moccasins were ready, she gave them to Kayak with her blessing. Kayak kissed her goodbye. Then, the very next morning, he ran away from home wearing the new moccasins.

As Kayak ran through the forest, he was watched from afar by Great Chief Glooskap, the mighty creator of the Wabanaki people, who was very fond of him. Glooskap guessed that besides being fast and strong, Kayak was probably kind and honest as well. He decided to test Kayak.

So Glooskap came down to the forest disguised as a weak old man. He limped along the trail just a little way ahead of Kayak and as the boy ran up, he dropped a little box in front of him. Kayak stopped to pick it up and was very tempted to open it, or to slip it into his pocket without saying anything, but instead he called out, "Kwahee! Kwahee! Grandfather! You have dropped your little box. Let me bring it to you."

"Thank you, kind boy," Glooskap replied in a shaky voice. "This box holds something very precious to me."

Kayak smiled at the old man and asked him whether he could tell where the trail would take him, since he had not run this way before.

The old man said, "This trail leads to a distant Micmac village. It's a very hard path, full of rocks and thorns." Then he sighed as he looked down at his

own bare feet, which were already sore and scarred from traveling.

Kayak immediately took off his lovely moccasins, saying, "Dear grandfather, your feet are bleeding already. Take my moccasins, for my feet are young and tough and I can run as fast as the deer."

As Kayak prepared to run on, the old man caught his sleeve and said to him, "Keep this box and care for it well." With that he disappeared.

Kayak was curious and opened the box. But to his disappointment, he saw lying there only a tiny doll made of sweetgrass, just a common doll such as any child might play with. "What could I possibly do with you?" he asked. "I don't play with such things now."

To his astonishment, a small whispering voice answered, "I am the servant of whoever carries me. Whatever you ask, I will do for you."

Now Kayak was very scared, for he knew that this doll must be magic, so the old man must have been a magician! Not knowing what else to do, he quickly tucked the doll back into the box and ran on till he came at last to the Micmac village.

The Micmac people welcomed Kayak and treated him kindly. Then they took him into the teepee of their chief, Magooch. The chief was out hunting, but sitting beside the fire was his only daughter. Straight away, Kayak fell in love with her, for she was very beautiful. An old squaw who was sitting nearby told him that the girl's name was Seboosis.

"Please tell Magooch that I am weary of being alone and I should like to take Seboosis for my wife," said Kayak.

"I will do as you ask," the old squaw replied, "but I fear that Magooch intends her to marry Toobe, a youth of our tribe."

When Magooch returned, the old woman told him of Kayak's offer of marriage and the chief agreed to meet him. Kayak stood at the entrance to the teepee and waited to be invited in further. Soon the chief summoned him. After they had talked for awhile, Magooch began to feel afraid of this young man, who clearly was very clever and had a mind and a will of his own. So he challenged Kayak with an impossible task. "That huge mountain on the horizon hinders my hunting. Go and move it and you shall marry my daughter," he said. He was sure that Kayak couldn't possibly achieve such a feat and would go away and bother him no more.

But Kayak smiled quietly and accepted the task. He waited until the sun had set, then, when no one was looking, he opened his box and called on his magical sweetgrass doll to help him.

That night, the air was filled with strange sounds that kept Magooch awake. When he stumbled out of his teepee at first light, he was stunned to find the mountain gone! But instead of being pleased, he was angry and afraid. For this youth clearly had great strength and he feared that his people would soon respect him more than their old chief. So he resolved to get rid of Kayak. He called him to his side and said, "Across the lake lives an enemy tribe that provokes us to fight. If you can successfully lead a war-party of my Micmac braves against them, you may marry my daughter." He knew how fierce and strong these warriors were and thought that Kayak would surely be killed.

When they heard about Magooch's plan, the Micmac braves were afraid that they were being sent to their deaths and they held back from joining Kayak. But the young man told them not to worry, for he would happily go to fight the enemy on his own.

So Kayak set out alone, and the Micmac people waited in their village. Across the lake they could hear the battle rage for hours. Then at last a great silence fell. Everyone was sure that Kayak was dead and they mourned the loss of such a brave youth. Only Magooch was pleased. He started to prepare a wedding feast for Seboosis and Toobe, even though his daughter was weeping for Kayak.

When the wedding feast was ready, Magooch cried out, "Let the bridegroom come forth!" Seboosis turned away, dreading the sight of Toobe. But when she heard a strong voice call out, "I am here, my father, to claim Seboosis as my bride," she turned around in amazement. There stood Kayak, brave and strong and laughing with delight.

Of course, Magooch had to keep his promise, so Kayak was married to Seboosis. After the wedding he put the sweetgrass doll safely back in her box, and thanked from the bottom of his happy heart the mysterious old man who wore the moccasins so lovingly made by his mother. "Now I have all I need, I shall not use the doll again," he thought.

From his home in the skies, Glooskap looked down at the Micmac village and smiled at Kayak's happiness as he smoked his great pipe.

SNOT-NOSE

FRENCH

Beside a river in a land now hard to imagine, there once lived an old widow with three sons. The two older boys were bright and hardworking, but the youngest, Snot-Nose, had only one idea at a time and was scarcely able even to learn his prayers. Each morning he said simply, "Lord, I'm getting up," and at night, "Lord, I'm going to bed."

The family lived together in peace, managing to grow just enough to eat, until one cold day in March when rains fell on the melting snow and there was a great flood. Everything they owned was washed away in the waters.

Soon after this disaster a huge man on a massive horse rode by looking for a servant. "I'll take your eldest son with me," he said to the mother. "That will be one less mouth for you to feed."

Before they left, the man, who had eyes like a pig, said, "I'll hire him for a year for thirty crowns, until the cuckoo sings his first song next April. He will be fed on one egg a day and as much bread as he can spread with the egg. He must also feed my bitch, who will go to work with him each day. He must not return from the fields until she is ready. Is that clear? I'll keep my part of the bargain and he must keep his. And he'd better not complain that he's unhappy, or I'll whip him soundly and send him packing! Those are my conditions. If the first lad doesn't satisfy me, I'll come back for your next son."

The widow wept as the mean-looking fellow rode off with her son, for she had guessed his wickedness. He was a cruel lowland ogre.

Though the boy was hungry when they arrived at the ogre's farm, he was not fed till the next day, when he was given a hard-boiled egg. This he could spread on nothing larger than a tiny crust. The ogre's wife threw the bread to him. She was a hideous creature with one long red tooth that reached down to her chin. Then the boy was sent off to work with instructions to plow a huge field and he was forbidden to return before the bitch was ready. So he didn't get home till night.

"You don't look very happy," said the ogre.

"How can I be happy when I'm exhausted and hungry?" the boy replied.

"So, you won't keep our bargain, you lazy brute!" the ogre shouted, while his wife came over with a whip to thrash him.

Imagine the mother's shock when her poor boy was returned. How she regretted entering into such a bond with this horrible ogre! But she could not get out of it and as the sun set over the river, her second son was carried off. He fared no better than his brother. He could hardly stand when he got back from plowing the vast field, watched by the red-eyed bitch that begged for his food.

He was starving even before he gave a crust to the animal, for he too was unable to make a hard-boiled egg spread over much bread. So he complained miserably when he came back in the darkness to the ogre's kitchen. He too was whipped and returned home.

Snot-Nose was filled with anger when he saw the fate of his second brother. "I'll punish that ogre for his cruelty," he said to himself. Though his mother begged that the ogre release her from the bargain, the man insisted on carrying off her youngest son. As the distressed mother tended the wounds of her other sons, she prayed for the youngest, who would be so helpless against such a monster!

Snot-Nose was treated exactly like his brothers, but he was determined to outwit the ogre and punish him for hurting them. So he jumped out of bed as soon as he heard the cock crow. He fetched his own egg from the coop and with a feather painted a whole loaf with the egg, before the ogre's wife had time to boil it. The ogre could do nothing. Then Snot-Nose set off for the fields with the red-eyed bitch at his heels. He grabbed her by the collar, saying, "If I've got to feed you, then you have to earn your food." He yoked the bitch to the oxen and made her plow all day. How eager the poor creature was to go home by mid-afternoon! So Snot-Nose went back early, whistling blithely as he entered the farmyard.

The ogre and his wife were furious, but they could not deny that the bargain had been kept. They smelt trouble and already they wanted to get rid of the lad. But they couldn't send him away till the cuckoo sang in April. The stupid ogre tried desperately to think of a plan, but his head was usually heavy with drink.

However, early one morning when Snot-Nose came to him, singing happily, to find out his day's task, the scoundrel said, "No plowing today, my lad. I want you to cut two bundles of wood for me. One must be quite straight and the other as crooked as a dog's leg. Have them ready in an hour, or else you'll suffer!"

The ogress approved of his plan, for the forest was many miles away. She knew the boy couldn't possibly get there in an hour, let alone get back with the wood cut. And there was no other forest near the farm.

How wrong the couple were! For a beautiful grove of poplars lined the path to the farm, and beyond it lay a vineyard, both of which the ogre had planted with great pride. Snot-Nose knew this, of course, and took great delight in felling every poplar and hacking down every vine.

"Here are your bundles of wood, Master. No branches are straighter than these poplars and none so crooked as these vines."

The ogre and his wife groaned and raged but could do nothing to protest. The boy had kept to the bargain yet again. How could they get rid of him? For they must honor their side of the bargain too. They must not admit to being unhappy either. So life went on for a few more weeks, with Snot-Nose tricking his master at every turn.

The ogress grew impatient with her stupid husband and urged him to think of a way to trap Snot-Nose. "Give him a really hard job, like laying a road from the forest to our own farmyard. That he could never do."

The next morning when Snot-Nose came down to breakfast with a gleam in his eye, the ogre shouted, "Enough of this holiday! It's time now for work. I want a road built from the woods to my back door, a beautiful white, smooth road, seven miles long. Have it finished by evening."

After the boy had set off for the woods, the ogre and ogress sat in the garden drinking wine all day and dozing. They were looking forward to getting rid of their troublesome young servant. Snot-Nose actually had to wake them when he came back in the evening.

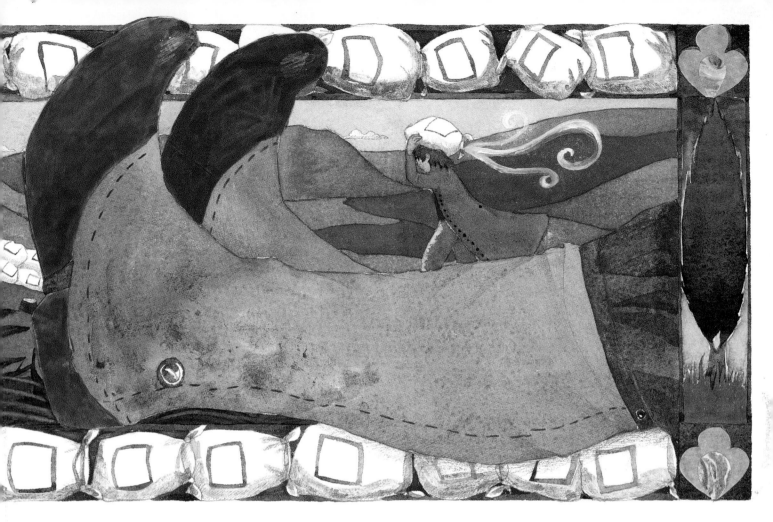

"Come and see your road," he shouted in the ogre's ear. Snot-Nose led him round the back of the house. The ogre was stunned with fury when he saw what the boy had done. The white road was there, for sure – it had been made out of the thousands of bags of white flour that the ogre kept in his many barns. But even now, he could not explode with rage. He must not complain or seem unhappy, though he was ready to smash his own head against the barn wall! As for Snot-Nose, he thought of his mother and brothers and was content.

But soon the ogre and his wife conjured up another task. "Take the cows out of the barn," the mad ogre bellowed, "without opening the door. And put them in the meadow without opening the gate." He thought this was a brilliant plot. This would fox the boy! "Do it within the hour," the ogre added.

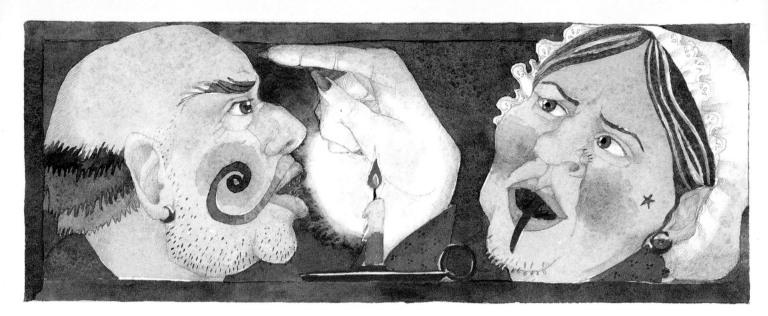

Snot-Nose had no other thought but revenge. His love for his mother and brothers gave him courage. So he immediately set about his task and within an hour called his master to see the results. The ogre could not believe his eyes. The lad had killed every one of his cows, cut them into small pieces and put them in the meadow. The barn door and meadow gate were closed, for he had thrown the meat out through the little window and over the wall of the meadow! How else could he have done it?

The two ogres screamed with fury, but they had to insist that they were quite satisfied with his work. When Snot-Nose was in bed, sleeping peacefully, they plotted all night to destroy him. Just before dawn, they hit on an idea that could not fail. "Let us send him to our cousin Babouane. She'll not be fooled by the young stripling. She'll just devour him in one mouthful," gloated the ogress. "So she will," chuckled her husband. "So she will." Satisfied that they had found a sure way of getting rid of Snot-Nose, the couple went happily to bed and soon fell into a snoring sleep.

When he woke at noon, the ogre sent for Snot-Nose and commanded him, "Here's your job for today. Take my sixty pigs to forage for acorns in Babouane's wood."

So the boy set off, following the red-eyed bitch till they came to a clearing where he saw a shepherdess guarding her sheep.

"Where are you going?" the shepherdess asked.

"To Babouane's wood to find acorns," Snot-Nose replied.

"You'll never come back," said the shepherdess in terror. "She will eat you for sure."

"If you will give me a cheese, all will be well," Snot-Nose urged.

So the shepherdess went to her hut and brought Snot-Nose one of her cheeses. With the cheese in his hand, Snot-Nose went on till he came to a goatherd with his flock of goats.

"Where are you going?" the goatherd asked.

"To Babouane's wood to find acorns," responded the boy.

"Don't go there!" warned the goatherd. "She'll devour you. No one ever returns from her wood."

"If I take this puffball with me, all will be well," Snot-Nose said, as he bent to pick the fungus.

Off he went with cheese and puffball till he met a hunter, who asked him, "Where are you going, my boy?"

"I'm off to Babouane's wood to find acorns," Snot-Nose said confidently.

"Go somewhere else, anywhere but there!" insisted the hunter. "She'll surely kill you."

"Not if you let me borrow your gun," suggested Snot-Nose.

"If you'll get rid of that evil sorceress, you can have my gun," the hunter replied quickly.

Off went Snot-Nose with cheese and puffball and gun, right to the heart of Babouane's terrible forest. There she was, large, ferocious and mean. Her pigs were bigger than houses.

"I demand pasture for my pigs," Snot-Nose challenged her.

"If you prove stronger than me, you can have my pigs as well," she laughed. "But if I prove stronger than you, I take all yours." And the foul ogress grinned from ear to ear. "But what's that round thing like a cheese on your arm?" she continued.

"That's why they call me Snot-Nose," he answered. "I sometimes blow my nose on my sleeve."

"What must it be like when you spit!" Babouane groaned.

"Just watch me," said Snot-Nose and he cleared his throat and pretended to spit. As he did so, he fired lead from the gun at the ogress. Thick-skinned though she was, the lead stung her flesh like thousands of burning needles.

"By the devil," she exploded, "you certainly are powerful! But watch me now." Babouane bent down, picked up a stone and squeezed it so hard that it crumbled into gravel. For the first time, Snot-Nose began to feel scared, but he knew just what to do next.

"That's nothing," boasted Snot-Nose. "Watch me!" With that he too bent down but grasped the puffball instead of a stone. He squeezed it till it puffed into powder.

Babouane stared at him in astonishment. "All right, I grant it, you are stronger than me, and cleverer than my cousins. This wood is yours, take it and my pigs too. Goodbye!" And the coward was off, as fast as she could run on her short, ugly legs.

Snot-Nose herded her pigs before him to market, where they sold like

hot-cakes. No one had seen such huge creatures before. By the end of the day, he had made a great deal of money. With gold in his pockets, he set off for the ogre's farm.

When the ogre and ogress realized that they had been outwitted yet again, they were desperate. "We still have to keep him till the first cuckoo sings in April," the ogress lamented.

"Ah! I know just what we'll do," the ogre announced. "Bring me some tar and feathers."

Next morning Snot-Nose woke to the sound of the cuckoo. "How can that be?" he wondered, as he picked up his gun and went down to the garden. There he saw a large, ugly bird making a terrible noise. He raised his gun and filled the bird with lead.

As the ogress fell, she broke her long, red tooth. The ogre came howling from behind the bushes, screaming, "You bloodthirsty cannibal – the devil take you!" With that he started to beat Snot-Nose, who jumped nimbly aside and struck the ogre with the barrel of his gun. But Snot-Nose was not cruel, nor was he stupid. So he just threw the ogre among the nettles. He picked up the broken tooth and put it on a thong around his neck and set off for the river. He was home by sunset and his mother greeted him, weeping for joy at his safe return.

As they sat round the fire that evening counting the gold, Snot-Nose told the story of his adventures exactly as I've told them to you. So you can be sure that this tale is true, though none of us saw these things happen.

THE MISTRESS OF FIRE

SELKUP

A long time ago, when the cold winds of winter swept across Siberia, the men of the Selkup people left their wives and children in their tents and set out for the forest to find food. One of the women had a young baby boy whom she looked after on her own. The weather grew steadily colder, and as evening fell, the woman went out to fetch some logs. Then she piled them in the hearth and lit a fire. She sat down beside it, rocking her son close to her body. But as the fire grew, it began to spit sparks and one fell on her small son and burned him. When her baby screamed in pain, she jumped up and shouted angrily at the fire.

"I feed you with logs and fill you with branches and yet you hurt my precious child!" she cried. "You'll not get anything else from me. I'll pour water all over you! I'll chop you in pieces!"

With that she put the boy in his cradle, picked up the axe and started hacking at the flames. Then she poured a pot of water over the fire, still screaming, "Now you won't burn my boy again! Now you can't harm anybody."

After this, she was so exhausted that she collapsed on the fur rug beside the cradle and glared angrily at the dark, smouldering hearth. As the tent became colder and colder, her baby started to cry and she began to realize just what she had done. Desperately she tried to rekindle the fire, but it refused to come to life. She breathed and blew into the embers, but it was hopeless.

Soon her little son's cries drove the woman to the tents of her neighbors, hoping to bring back a taper of fire. But when she arrived in their homes, their fires immediately died. Wherever she went, the fire went out. Then the other Selkup women knew that she must have offended the Mistress of Fire.

Weeping bitterly, the poor woman went back to her freezing tent to try to share her own body heat with her son. Because everyone's fire had gone out, it was dark and cold throughout the camp that night. No matter what she did, the woman could not stop her baby crying. She was almost at her wits' end, when a kind old woman lifted the flap and stepped inside the tent. "Let us see whether we can do anything to appease the Mistress of Fire," she said softly, as she too tried to create a spark by rubbing sticks together. For a while nothing happened, then there were just enough sparks to catch light to a piece of wool. Patiently the old woman added kindling wood, then through a faint glow in the middle of the flames she saw an ancient crone. As she attended to the fire, the crone's wrinkled face began to gleam. Then she spoke from the embers.

"You cannot have more fire," she said gently, "so labor no more. This foolish woman has dishonored me. She has cut my body and thrown water in my

bright face. She has injured me badly and she must suffer for it."

The old woman begged the crone, "I am sorry for my sister's folly, and so is she, but please do not make us all suffer cold and death because of her anger. Please spare us! Return the gift of your fire!"

The Mistress of Fire considered her words for some time before she spoke again. "Very well," she said, "I will not let you die. I will give you my fire again, but on one condition. I must have this woman's son as her gift. I will create new fire from his heart. Never again will she treat fire with such disrespect."

The mother shook with terror when she heard these words and she looked pleadingly at the old Selkup woman, who spoke to her kindly. "Because of you we are all doomed to death. Only you can save us now. There is no other way. You must give the Mistress of Fire your only son." But she too was shocked.

The mother's heart broke as she gave up her boy. As the Mistress of Fire took him in her warm hands, she looked at the women in the cold tent and said, "From now on, you people of the Selkups, I require that you never touch fire with any iron tools. Only with my permission, in terrible times, may you do so. This is my command. Make sure you never offend me again."

With those words she touched the dead logs in the hearth and straight away they leaped into life, curling up into the opening at the tent's top and out into the sky. Then the Mistress of Fire took the child with her into the flames.

The old woman tried to comfort the mother, saying, "Tonight a new legend has been born. Tonight fire was kindled from the heart of your child to save the Selkup people. This story will be on our lips for generations."

And to this day, the Selkup people tell this tale, especially when the waters freeze and they seek warmth by the fires in their tents.

THE HORSE
AND THE SWORD

ICELANDIC

Once upon a time there lived a king and queen who had just one son, whose name was Sigurd. They lived together happily until the queen became sick. None of the royal doctors could help her and soon she died. The king built a beautiful monument to his lost wife and he sat there and mourned for her each day.

One morning, as the king was sitting by the monument, a tall woman approached him. She told him that her name was Ingiborg and asked what he was doing. So the king told Ingiborg about his sorrow and when he had finished, she explained that she too was mourning, for her husband had just died. The two of them comforted one another and agreed to meet again.

Soon they became such good friends that they decided to marry.

Now the king became happy again and he returned to his favorite pastime of hunting in the great forest. One day he asked his son to go with him, but Sigurd preferred to stay at home. He had become very fond of Ingiborg, and he wanted to be near her.

So Sigurd told Ingiborg that he would not go hunting with his father the next day. She tried to force Sigurd to go, but he would not listen to her. When morning came, she said, "You will be very sorry that you have refused to do as I ask. But since you will not go out, you must hide under this bed. Lie absolutely still, until I call you."

Sigurd lay under the bed and soon he felt the ground shake and tremble like an earthquake. As he peeped out, he saw a great giantess wading to the palace, churning up the earth as she went.

"Good day, sister Ingiborg," he heard the giantess say. "Has Prince Sigurd stayed at home today?"

"Oh no," said his stepmother, "he is out hunting in the forest. Now come and eat the food I have prepared for you."

The giantess tore the meat apart and when she could eat no more, she thanked her sister and left. As she went out she asked again, "Are you quite sure that the prince is not here?"

Ingiborg again denied that Sigurd was at home and her sister left, churning up the earth as she went.

The next day Ingiborg again begged Sigurd to go out hunting with his father. But again he wanted to stay near her and refused to leave. So once more she told him to hide, this time under the table. "Don't move or even sneeze and don't come out until I call you," she ordered her stepson.

From his hiding place Sigurd again felt the earth move. Another giantess came, plowing up the earth as she approached the palace. "Has Prince Sigurd stayed at home today?" she began, as she sat down to the lamb and bread and beer that her sister had prepared for her.

"No, no, he is not here," Ingiborg insisted. "He has gone off to the forest with his father."

Once the food had been devoured, the giantess took her leave, asking yet again as she left, "Sister, are you quite certain that Prince Sigurd is not here?"

Ingiborg reassured her that he was out hunting and once the giantess was out of sight, she called the prince from his hiding place.

The next day the same thing happened – Sigurd refused to leave his stepmother's side, no matter how angrily she spoke to him. "You will just have to hide me again," he said to her as his father rode off. This time, Ingiborg hid him in a crack in the wall. Very soon, Sigurd felt the earth shake and he knew that a third giantess must be on her way.

In a monstrous voice the third sister greeted Ingiborg and demanded to know whether Prince Sigurd was at home. "No, no," Ingiborg insisted, "he has gone off to the forest hunting. He will not be home before nightfall."

So the giantess ate her lunch and then prepared to leave. But before she went she asked again, "Are you quite certain that the prince is not here?" Then she turned around and shouted at the top of her voice, "If you are within hearing, little Prince Sigurd, hear this curse! May you become withered and may your flesh burn. And may you have no rest till you find me!"

With these terrible words she strode off, and the earth trembled as she went.

When Sigurd came out of his hiding place, Ingiborg was horrified to find that his body was marked with burns and his flesh was withering. "Now you see what trouble your stubbornness has caused you!" she cried. "There is only one thing to do. You must take this ball of string and these three gold rings and leave this castle at once. Roll the string along the ground and follow it till you come to a cliff where a giantess stands. She will call down to you, 'Ah, here is Prince Sigurd! Tonight we shall cook him for supper!' Then you must reply with a greeting from me. Do not be frightened when she pulls you up with a hook and wrestles with you, for when you get tired, she will give you some wine to drink and this will help you to overcome her."

Sigurd listened carefully to these instructions and was ready to leave when Ingiborg added, "This will happen with each of my sisters, so be prepared. And heed this last thing. If my puppy should ever come to you, with tears running down his face, then you must hasten back here, for I will need you. Now off you go. Travel safely and never forget me."

With that Sigurd departed. He threw down the ball and it led him to the cliff where the first giantess stood, crying out, "Here is Prince Sigurd! Tonight we shall cook him for supper."

The boy was afraid, but he called back, "I bring greetings from your sister Ingiborg," and she threw down a large hook and pulled him to the cliff top. Then she challenged him to wrestle with her. Seeing that he grew tired, she offered him a drink from a strange horn, not knowing that this would bring back his strength. Now he wrestled even more powerfully until finally he threw her to the ground. Then he gave her the smallest ring to pacify her and went on his way.

He followed the ball of string to another cliff where the second and fiercer giantess stood. The same things happened as with her sister. Once Sigurd had wrestled her to the ground, refreshed by the drink in the strange horn, he gave her the second ring and followed the ball of string on to the last giantess.

The third and most terrible of the sisters stood towering over Sigurd on the cliff top. She too threatened to cook him for supper. Again he called out, "I bring greetings from your sister Ingiborg," so she too drew him up the cliff on a large hook.

"Now you must fight with me!" she shouted, and they wrestled till he could scarcely stand. But when he drank from her horn, he recovered once more and threw the terrible creature to the ground. Then, after he had given her the third and final ring, she said kindly, "Now you have overcome me, and must continue on your journey. You will come to a large lake where a young girl plays. Greet her by her name, Helga, and give her this golden ring. Now go and be lucky!"

With these words, she gave the ring back to Sigurd and he went on his way.

When he came to the lake, Sigurd met Helga and they played together till evening. At first, Helga would not invite Sigurd back to her home for the

night, for her father was a fierce giant and had forbidden any human to enter
his castle. But Sigurd insisted that he must come with her, so at last she agreed
to take him home. As they entered the castle, she waved her glove over Sigurd
and changed him into a bundle of wool. How afraid he was when the giant
came in sniffing loudly. "What can I smell?" he roared.

"It's only a bundle of wool, father," Helga replied and so Sigurd was safe.

When the giant left, Helga waved her glove over the ball of wool and Sigurd
regained his human form. Now he was curious to be shown all the rooms and
towers. So Helga took him from room to room, till they came to the last one.
"We are forbidden to go in here," the girl said, but Sigurd persuaded her to
open the door just a crack. Inside, he saw a splendid stallion. "What a
magnificent horse!" he exclaimed. "I must ride it, if only for a minute. And I
must try that sword," he called to Helga, "for I have never seen such a
splendid weapon!" Helga's heart was pounding as she tried to prevent Sigurd
from mounting the horse. "That is Gullfaxi, the Golden Mane. He is my
father's most precious horse," she explained. "And that is Gunnfioder, the
Battle Plume, his most valued sword. He will be in a rage if he knows they
have even been seen. So if you must ride the horse and try the sword, then go."

As Sigurd swung himself into the saddle, Helga also offered him a stick, a stone and a twig. "You had better have these too," she said. "They will protect you." Sigurd thanked her, but then rode swiftly away.

When Helga's father returned to find that his horse and sword were missing, he was furious. At once he raced after Sigurd. The young prince trembled with fear as he heard the giant following him, but he waited until he felt the giant's breath on his neck, then he dropped the twig on the path. Straight away a thick forest rose up and caught the giant in its branches, so that Sigurd could escape, but it didn't take the giant long to catch up. Sigurd waited until his pursuer could almost touch the tail of Gullfaxi, then he hit the stone with the stick and huge hailstones started to pelt the giant. This time he fell down dead.

By now, Sigurd was exhausted, so he stopped for a moment to rest. As he sat under a tree, his stepmother's puppy came running up to him, with tears running down his face. Sigurd took up the puppy, mounted Gullfaxi again and raced back to the castle. There he found Ingiborg in great danger, for some faithless menservants were about to kill her and take over the castle while his father lay sick in bed. Sigurd charged into the courtyard on his mighty horse and with the sword Gunnfioder he slew the servants with a few strokes and saved his stepmother. Together they went in to the king, who was so pleased to see his son safely returned that he began to get well immediately.

"Now I will ride back to the giant's castle on Gullfaxi to claim Helga as my bride," Sigurd announced. And so Prince Sigurd married Helga with great feasting and dancing and joy, and the couple lived in peace for many years.

HANS IN LUCK

GERMAN

There was once a youth called Hans who had served his master faithfully for seven years. At the end of that time, he came to his master and said, "Master, I have served you well and my task is finished. I want to go back home to my mother now. Please pay me what you owe me."

His master was sad to lose so good a servant but he immediately paid the lad generously and sent him on his way. His reward was a lump of gold as big as his head!

Hans wrapped his gold in a large handkerchief and took to the road with the burden resting on his broad shoulders. He was soon approached by a man on horseback. As he watched the man canter towards him, Hans exclaimed, "How splendid to ride on a horse! You don't trip over sticks or stones and never wear out your shoes."

The horseman heard this and called to him, "Greetings! Why on earth do you stumble along on foot?"

Hans sighed as he replied, "Oh, I should prefer to ride, but I have this huge lump of gold to carry and it sits so heavily on my shoulders."

"Well then," the rider said, "why don't you exchange your burden for my horse? Then you can ride home as fast as the wind."

So Hans handed over his lump of gold to the man and mounted the horse with great delight. The rider had instructed him that whenever he wanted the horse to go fast, he must shout "whooah" and click his tongue. So Hans sat proudly in the saddle as the horse cantered off and he clicked his tongue and called "whooah." But the horse galloped out of control and soon poor Hans was thrown to the ground. He lay there quite dazed while a passing farmer caught his horse and brought it back to him.

"You'd be better off with my cow, my lad," said the farmer, "for then you could just amble along safely and enjoy the morning air and sunshine."

"You're right," replied Hans, rubbing his bruises. "Then let us exchange these animals right now."

Before Hans could count to ten, the farmer was up on the saddle and had galloped away, while the cow looked on patiently. Hans started to walk along beside his cow, thinking how lucky he was to have such a ready source of milk and butter. "I will never go hungry," he thought contentedly.

When he reached the next inn he stopped for a beer and ate the food that he had brought for the journey home to his mother. By mid-afternoon the sun was beating down on him and he grew very thirsty. So he stopped and said to his cow, "I am parched with the heat. So you must give me your milk now, good cow." He fastened the cow to a withered tree stump and tried to milk her, using his hat for a bucket. But no matter how he labored, not a drop of milk would come from the barren cow. Finally, she grew tired of his efforts and kicked Hans hard.

Just then a butcher passed by, pushing a pig in a cart. When he saw Hans he stopped and offered the weary youth a drink from his flask. "You have been tricked with that beast," he advised Hans. "She's fit only for the plow. Or for the butcher's knife," he added quickly.

"That seems to be true," admitted Hans. "But I don't like beef and I couldn't possibly carry a whole cow home. Now your pig would be a different matter."

"Very well, take my pig and enjoy your sausages!" responded the farmer. "I'm happy with either beast, so let's exchange them."

Hans felt so blessed by his good fortune that he went on his way with the pig, whistling merrily. He was soon joined by a young boy carrying a goose under his arm.

"Just feel this goose," he urged Hans. "What a juicy creature it is. It has been fattened for eight weeks for a christening feast. How the fat will run down our chins when we eat this one!"

"My pig will make a good feast too," replied Hans. Then he noticed that the youth was looking round him uneasily.

"It might be a good pig," the boy admitted, "but I've just passed through a village where the mayor's own pig had been stolen. They are now on the lookout for anyone traveling with a pig. You could end up in jail. You'd better be careful."

Hans was very afraid when he heard this and wondered what he could do to

protect himself. Then the boy with the goose said to him, "Listen, my friend. I know these roads and bypaths and I will be safe with the pig. So you take my goose instead, since you are a stranger in these parts."

"How lucky I am," Hans reflected. "Every time trouble comes, I manage to avoid it. Things are going so well today!"

He set off with his goose under his arm, thinking of the feast he would have with his mother and how they would sleep on soft, feather pillows. His daydream was interrupted by a scissor-grinder who wheeled along his grinding barrow singing at the top of his voice:

I grind and grind the scissors sharp and bright,
While the wind blows roughly both day and night.

He stopped when he saw Hans and greeted him merrily.

"How contented you seem," Hans said. "You must enjoy sharpening scissors and you must make a good living at it."

"Oh yes, indeed," the grinder replied. "Every day when I put my hand in my pocket, I pull out more gold! So prosperous is my trade. Now where did you get that fat goose, may I ask?"

"I exchanged it for a pig," Hans answered.

"And where did you get the pig from?" the grinder persisted.

"That I exchanged for a cow," said Hans.

"And the cow?"

"In exchange for a horse."

"And the horse?"

"That I exchanged for a most burdensome lump of gold as big as my head," Hans explained.

"Where on earth did you get such a lump of gold from?" asked the grinder.

"My master gave me that as reward for my seven years of service."

"You've certainly done well," encouraged the grinder, "but you will not have succeeded fully until you can hear money jingling in your pockets when you move. Then you will be most fortunate." With that the grinder watched silently as Hans considered his words.

"Can you tell me how to do that?" he asked.

"Oh yes, I can. All you need is a grindstone like mine. It does all the work for you. Mine is a little chipped but it will do you fine. Perhaps you could give me your goose in exchange?" the grinder suggested.

"This is certainly my lucky day! Here, take my goose and give me your

stone and I shall indeed be successful," Hans cried out, as the grinder looked

around for a large stone nearby. This he gave to Hans, who could hardly move

with it. Then the grinder went on his way.

"I must have been blessed at birth," Hans thought. "I must have been born

on a Sunday at least, to be so fortunate as this." And he sang as he struggled

with the heavy stone. On he went until he felt dreadfully tired, weighed

down as he was by his burden. So when he came to a well, he stopped to

drink. He placed his stone carefully on the edge while he drank. But before he knew it, he had nudged the stone over the side and it fell into the well with a loud splash. Hans stood looking down into the dark depths and his heart sang with joy. "What a relief!" he exclaimed. "That stone was so heavy to carry and now God has delivered me from its burden and I can run home quite free!"

With that Hans jumped for joy and ran all the way home to his mother.

THE CHANGELING
OF LLANFABON

WELSH

Long, long ago in a farmhouse in the parish of Llanfabon, there lived a widow with her only son. His name was Pryderi, which means "loss," and his mother loved him more than words can tell. By the time he was three years old, Pryderi was a most beautiful and clever boy.

Now in those days, the land of Wales was full of faeries, and these faeries were real mischief-makers. They often kept the people awake with their music all night long. They played tricks on the farmers by day and led them into the bogs with their false lights after dark. And there was nothing they liked better than to steal human children from their beds at night and take them away to the faery realm. The widow knew this, so she always guarded her son carefully.

One winter's evening, the widow heard her cows calling out in distress from the barn, so she rushed to see what the trouble was. She was in such a hurry that she forgot to protect her son by placing the fire tongs crosswise over his bed. When she reached the barn, the woman was mystified to find the cows calm and safe. Then, as she went back to the house, she remembered the faeries and was suddenly filled with terror. She raced inside to the boy's bed, afraid to find it empty. But there was her child, and he smiled at her as he called out, "Mother!"

But there was something not quite right about the boy. "You seem strange, my darling," she said. "What do you mean, mother? I am your own dear son," he answered cheerfully. Still, something troubled her. As the days went by, the boy became bad-tempered and spiteful. She also noticed that he seemed to grow more and more ugly.

So fearful was the widow that she went to see the Wise Man of Llanfabon. He was the only man able to live in the Castle of the Night, which was built from the stones of the ruined church. Everyone else had been afraid to live there. The Wise Man of Llanfabon understood dark mysteries. The widow felt that if anyone could help her, he could.

When the Wise Man of Llanfabon had heard what the widow had to say, he responded solemnly, "I think I can help you. But you must follow my instructions exactly. Tomorrow at noon, brew some beer in an eggshell. The boy will watch you carefully, but do not attend to him. Only when he asks you what you are doing, tell him that you are brewing beer for the harvesters. Then make a note of his reply but pretend not to hear him. Put him to bed as usual, then come to me again."

The widow did just as she had been told. The boy stood watching her intently as she brewed the beer. Finally, he asked what she was doing.

"I'm brewing beer for the harvesters," she explained, and in response he whispered:

Today I am old, as old as the hill, yet I lived long before I was born.
That oak tree began before the old mill, yet I played with it still as an acorn.
But never did I see the shell of a hen brewing beer for the thirsty harvestmen.

The woman listened carefully, as the Wise Man of Llanfabon had told her. Then she asked, "Did you say something, Pryderi?" as though she had not heard him. The boy shouted back angrily, "Oh, nothing at all, mother, nothing at all."

That night, the widow put the child to bed and waited patiently until he was sound asleep. Then she went back across the hills to the Wise Man. She told him the strange things she had heard the boy say and the old man listened with a sad face. "Yes, yes, I thought so. But I think I can help you, if you do exactly as I say. In four days' time, the moon will be full. At the stroke of midnight, you must go to where the four roads cross at the Ford of the Bell. Hide there with care, for you will be in great peril if you are seen. The next day, come and report to me what happens."

The widow did exactly as the Wise Man had instructed her. As soon as midnight struck, she went to the Ford of the Bell and hid herself at the crossroads. At first the moon shone like day in the gloomy night, but suddenly the clouds covered it and, in the darkness, she heard the most exquisite music approaching from afar. As it came nearer, she saw a marvelous procession of faeries dancing towards her. While the faeries danced past her, the moon

appeared and she was able to see them clearly. She almost swooned with the beauty of the music, but her pleasure turned to pain when she saw, in the very midst of the dancers, her own dear child, Pryderi. She held her breath, her heart almost bursting as she waited patiently for the procession to pass by. When the music was a faint murmur and then only a memory, she dragged herself home and lay in her bed fearfully till morning.

As soon as day broke, she hurried back to the Wise Man of Llanfabon, who knew what she had to tell him as soon as he saw her face. "Do not worry," he comforted her. "I can help you if you do as I say." Then he reached for a strange, leather-bound book which he read in silence. After a while, he looked up and said, "You have a most difficult task, for you must find a pure black hen, without even a single white feather. You must then light a fire with peat and bake the hen in the flames till the last feather is consumed. You must close every passageway, every hole in your house while you do this, except the chimney. Keep your eyes on the hen till the very end and on no account look at the changeling boy."

The woman set out on her quest to find a pure black hen. Day after day she wandered the hills and woods, searching and asking, hoping and despairing, until finally she found a jet-black hen many miles from Llanfabon.

During this time the changeling child grew uglier and uglier and she found it more and more difficult to live with him. But once she found the hen, she lit the fire and baked it in the flames while the boy watched. All the time she did just as the Wise Man of Llanfabon had instructed her, keeping her eyes on the hen until the very last feather began to burn. By then, the heat was so great that she fainted.

When the widow woke, she found that the changeling had disappeared.

Then she thought she could hear the delicious music that she had heard at the Ford of the Bell and, in the midst of the music, she heard something still more beautiful. Her own son's voice was calling out, "Mother, mother! Where are you?"

The widow rushed outside and there, just a few paces from her door, she saw her child, who ran to her with joy. His eyes were bright and his laugh was like a trickling stream. She caught him in her arms and hugged him till he could scarcely breathe!

"Where have you been all this time?" she asked urgently.

"Oh, somewhere quite lovely, mother," Pryderi replied. "Just listening to lovely music!"

He was never able to say more than this, no matter how much she questioned him. He soon grew robust and strong and played and worked happily all his life. But he never quite forgot the magical music of the faeries, and nor did his mother.

THE BOY AND
THE SEEDPOD CANOE

MAORI

This story begins with a man and his wife who lived long ago. One day the wife suddenly became hungry for birds. She would not eat anything else, and soon she started to grow pale and weak. Every day, she begged her husband to trap a bird for her. Of course, it was a baby growing inside her that made her feel this way.

The man wanted to satisfy his wife's longing, so he went to the forest and caught two birds. One was a white heron and the other was a huia bird. When he brought them home, he was very surprised to find that his wife would not cook and eat them, despite her craving. Instead, she kept them near her as pets.

While her baby grew inside her, the wife looked after the two birds carefully. During this time, her husband left her and went back to his own people. So she lived alone and when the time was ready, she gave birth to a baby boy. She loved her baby so dearly that she named him Tautini-awhitia, which means "cherished for many years."

Tautini-awhitia was very strong and loved to play with his friends at every kind of sport, especially bird-catching. Before long, he was so skillful at whatever he attempted that the other boys became jealous of him. So one day they began to taunt him, saying, "Tautini-awhitia wins every game, but we don't care because he hasn't got a father!"

Then the boy went straight home to his mother in tears and demanded to know where his father was. "Your father has gone a long way away, beyond the sunrise," she replied. "You must look in that direction if you want to find him."

The boy went straight to the forest and found the pod of the rewerewa tree. He took it to the stream and floated it and discovered that it could move through the water without tipping over. So he went home to his mother and said, "I have found a way to travel beyond the rising of the sun. I will go there to find my father." His rewerewa pod was the first Maori canoe.

The boy's mother was pleased by his skill and admired his canoe. Then she begged him to wait while she prepared food for his journey. But her son would not listen to her, for he was eager to be off. So he launched his seedpod boat into the waters of the sea and paddled away. His mother wept as he departed. As he moved out of sight, she stood on the shore and chanted a spell for his safe journey. She stayed there quietly until long after the canoe had disappeared.

Tautini-awhitia paddled his canoe for many days, until at last he saw a village

by the shore. He paddled quietly up to the beach and hid his canoe in the sand. Then he went into the village to see if he could find his father. The children all gathered round to look at him and they laughed at him unkindly. Then one of the older boys told him to come back to his family home, to be their servant. When the father of the family saw Tautini-awhitia, he said, "Take him to sleep in the cookhouse – that's a good enough place for a servant." In this way the boy was shamed, but his spirit was not crushed.

When all the children were playing the next day, Tautini-awhitia crept off into the forest alone and caught some birds. He took them back to the cookhouse in secret. They were the very same birds that he had longed for when he was still in his mother's belly! He spoke with the birds and taught them to speak too. First he said to the huia bird, "I will tell you what you must say. You must say, 'The fire does not burn, the fire is not burning! It is so dark, so dark, so dark!'" Then he said to the white heron, "I will tell you

what you must say too. You must say, 'The fire does not burn, the fire is not burning! But the light shines! The light shines!'"

That night when it was quite dark, Tautini-awhitia left the cookhouse and gazed into the house of his father. Everyone was sleeping inside, so he crept in and put his birds in their cage among the dead ashes of the fireplace. In the midst of the dark and the silence, the huia bird suddenly cried, "The fire does not burn! The fire is not burning! It is so dark, so dark, so dark!" Then the white heron cried out, "The fire does not burn! The fire is not burning! But the light shines! The light shines!"

The men were all amazed and leaped up to inspect the speaking birds. Then the father of Tautini-awhitia came near to the boy crouching by the fireplace and said, "This is my son. He has proved this to me, because these are the very same birds that his mother longed for."

And the father embraced his brave son and welcomed him into his home.

CINDERELLO

GREEK

Once upon a time there was a boy, the only son of his mother, who refused to go outside but sat all day near the hearth among the cinders, so that he was given the name Cinderello. Every day his mother urged him to go out to play, but he would not. Then one morning she pleaded with him so much that at last Cinderello said, "I will go out, mother, if you will give me a ten-lepton piece."

"So much money just to get you outside?" his mother said crossly. But she was so glad that he would go that she gave him the money.

Cinderello wandered through the village and came across a group of boys who were treating a dog most cruelly. "If you let me take the dog home, I will give you this ten-lepton piece," he said. The boys quickly accepted his offer, so he called the dog and took it home, to feed and love it.

For weeks he again refused to go out. Then one day he said, "Very well, I will go out, mother, if you will give me another ten-lepton piece." Of course, his mother gave in again and off he went with the money. As he came near the woods, he saw another group of boys being unkind to a stray cat. "If you will let me have that cat, I will give you this ten-lepton piece," the boy said. The leader of the group agreed and the boy went home happily with his cat.

But the weeks passed and again Cinderello refused to go outside. Finally, his mother begged him so much that he said, "All right, I will go out, mother, but only if you will give me one more ten-lepton piece."

And because she was weary of seeing him in the ashes every day, his mother gave him the money.

Once Cinderello was in the woods, he met a gang of boys who were tormenting a little snake. He cried out to them, "If you will only give me that snake, I will let you have my ten-lepton piece." Gladly the boys let him take the snake home and went off with the money.

Cinderello loved his animals and tended to their every need till they were fully grown. Then one day the snake asked if he could return to his own home.

"Of course," said Cinderello, "and I will accompany you."

"Very well," said the snake, "but only remember that when we reach my home, hundreds of snakes will surround you. Do not worry. Let them be, and I will call them off. When my father hears how you helped me, he will want to heap gifts upon you. But be sure to ask only for the ring under his tongue. Nothing else. Then all will be well."

So they set off for the snake's kingdom, Cinderello, the cat and the dog, with the snake worming its way behind them. When they arrived, Cinderello was indeed surrounded by thousands of snakes, but he let them be until they were called off. When the King of the Snakes came forward, his snake-friend said, "Dear father, this is Cinderello, the boy who saved my life!"

"I am most grateful," the King of the Snakes said warmly, "so you must choose a gift. Take anything you want from my kingdom."

Cinderello asked only for the ring under the king's tongue, which was given to him at once. He then said goodbye to his dear snake and set off home.

Now it was a hot day and the road was long. Soon Cinderello began to feel hungry and thirsty. "How foolish I have been," he thought. "Here I am on a lonely road with nothing to eat or drink and all I asked for was a silly ring!" With that he threw the ring on the ground in disgust. How amazed he was when out of the ring stepped a marvelous, tall blackamoor, who bowed before him and asked, "What shall I bring you, my lord of the ring? Your wish is my command."

At first, Cinderello was too astonished to speak. Then he remembered how hungry he was, so he asked for bread and water. When he had feasted, the blackamoor stepped back into the ring and Cinderello took to the road refreshed.

After he had been home for some time, he said to his mother one day, "Mother, I would like to marry the king's daughter. Please go to his castle and tell him that I ask for her hand in marriage."

So his mother gained audience with the king and after he had heard her request he said, "Your son can marry my daughter only if he can feed my whole army in one meal. Tell him to come to feed them in the marketplace in forty days."

Cinderello bided his time and then on the fortieth day he went with his
ring to the marketplace. When the army began to ride in before the king,
he instructed the blackamoor of the ring to provide food for all the men.
Immediately the blackamoor produced a huge banquet and the men ate their
fill. After this, the king again spoke to Cinderello's mother.

"If your son would marry my daughter," he said, "he must build a road of gold from your own door to mine. He must do this, too, in forty days."

Then Cinderello again bided his time until the fortieth day, when he struck his ring and bade the blackamoor build a road of gold from his own door to the king's. Immediately the road appeared, glittering in the sun. The king's daughter rejoiced.

But the king called for Cinderello's mother once more and said, "This is the third and last task for your son. If he would marry my daughter, he must build a palace next to mine, but a palace that is far more splendid. This he must do in forty days."

Cinderello bided his time till the fortieth morning, and when the king opened his eyes and looked out of his palace window, he saw the most astounding palace, more glorious than he could ever have imagined. He sent for Cinderello and he sent for his daughter and arranged a magnificent wedding for the young couple. They lived happily together in the splendid new palace and the king appointed another blackamoor to guard them.

However, this false blackamoor was jealous of Cinderello and persuaded the new bride to discover the source of his power. When he heard about the ring, he urged her to bring it to him so that he could admire it for himself. The innocent girl did as he asked, without stopping to think that he might use it against them. But of course the moment he had the jewel in his hands, he called forth the good blackamoor of the ring.

"I too am a blackamoor and I deserve more than this puny Cinderello," the false blackamoor cried. "So take the wretch out into the streets while he is still asleep and move this palace with me and the bride in it down to the bottom of the sea, where I will live in great luxury." Then he hid the ring under his tongue, so that no one could take it from him.

This was done in the twinkling of an eye, and poor Cinderello woke up in the street in front of his mother's house. He was soon comforted by his old friends the dog and cat, and then the animals talked together about how they could help their kind master. They set off, the cat astride the dog's back, and they swam out to sea and down under the waves. There the cat pounced on a mouse-bride on her way to her wedding and threatened not to release her until the other mice brought the ring back from under the blackamoor's tongue. The clever mouse-bridegroom took honey and mustard and with his tail put them in the nostrils of the sleeping blackamoor, who woke with a mighty sneeze, so that the ring flew across the room. Another mouse quickly snatched it up and rushed back to the cat with it. The cat jumped on to the dog's back and they swam back to the shore. The dog was curious to see the ring, but as the cat passed it to him, he dropped it into the sea.

The poor animals could not believe their bad
luck. Sadly they went back to Cinderello with the
tale of their adventures. All of them were heartbroken, and Cinderello pined
for his lost bride.

Then one morning as the three friends paced along the shore, the cat went
mewing up to a fisherman who was emptying his nets. Since she mewed so
sadly, the fisherman threw her a fish. Imagine her surprise when, inside the
gut of the fish, she found the ring that had fallen into the sea! With the ring
under her tongue she bounded back to her master. At once, Cinderello struck
the ring and called up the good blackamoor, who was delighted to be back in

his service. "Please go to the depths of the sea," Cinderello commanded, "and bring back the palace we made that was stolen from me. Bring it back with my bride safely inside."

No sooner had he asked than the palace was restored to its place. The king slew the false blackamoor and the happy bride was reunited with her bride-groom. The cat and dog jumped with glee at the celebrations and the young couple danced all night.

MOSES AND THE FAITHFUL MIDWIVES

BIBLICAL

Long, long ago, the people of Israel were taken into slavery in the land of Egypt. Their masters treated them badly, and they had to spend all day making bricks for mighty palaces. But despite this and the many other hardships they were made to suffer, they had a great number of children and even seemed to thrive in their exile. Soon their masters became jealous of them. They began to fear that with so many children being born to them, the Israelites would one day rebel and claim the land of Egypt for themselves. So they urged their Pharaoh to punish the Israelites by killing all the baby boys that were born to them. In this way they hoped that the Israelites would never have enough men to fight them.

Pharaoh consulted with his counselors and they decided that the midwives who assisted the birth of the children should be told to kill the baby boys at birth. So Pharaoh sent for the two midwives, Jochebed and her young daughter Miriam, and he said to them, "You two are the ones who deliver the babies born to your people. From now on, you must kill every baby boy as soon as he is born. You will be punished severely if you do not do as I command."

Miriam cried and Jochebed grieved at the Pharaoh's terrible command. "How can we destroy the new life of our children with such cruelty?" they asked each other. "No, despite the danger, we will spare them." And they assured each other that God would protect them.

When Pharaoh saw that his plan was not working, he again sent for his counselors. This time they were more fierce than before. "There is no point trying to make these women kill the babies for us. We must send our messengers to all the Israelite homes to let us know when babies are to be born, and then we must send our soldiers to take the children and to cast them into the waters to drown them." Pharaoh saw that this was done and many baby boys lost their lives in the sea and the rivers.

By now, Jochebed the midwife was very old, but Miriam was still a young woman. One day, Jochebed discovered that she was pregnant and Miriam dreamed that the child carried in her mother's womb would be a great man. He would save the Israelite people from their slavery and lead them to their own country.

As the days went by, Jochebed became a young and beautiful woman again and gave birth to her child with ease. The baby born to her was a most precious boy and she hid him from the soldiers who would kill him. When the baby

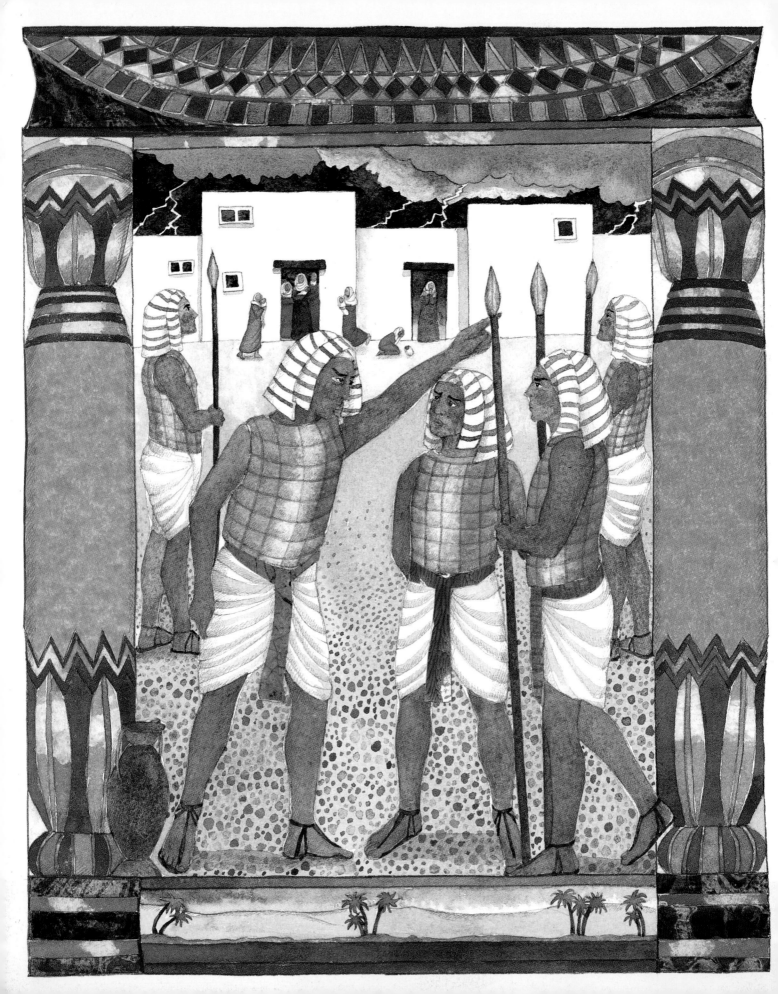

was only three days old, he could already speak and as he lay in his mother's arms, a glorious light shone around him. Jochebed could see that he was indeed a special child with a special fate.

One day the baby's father said, "We cannot hide this child any longer, for we are all in great danger from the soldiers who keep watch over us. If he is found, not only will he be killed, but you his mother, his brother Aaron and his sister Miriam too. So we must trust him to God and expose him to his fate."

Jochebed was filled with anguish at these words and wept for her boy. "I cannot let him die," she said. "We must find a way to save him. I will weave him a basket of rushes and it will be an ark for him in the waters."

So his mother wove a basket, lovingly, and lined it with soft clay and spread black pitch on the outside to make it waterproof for her child. She wrapped her boy in a blanket and covered him with warm cloth and took the little ark to the River Nile. There she found a hiding place among the bulrushes and set the basket afloat in the waters of the great river. With tears in her eyes, she said, "My dearest baby! I do not abandon you to the river, but I deliver you into the hands of Almighty God."

Then she turned to her daughter Miriam who stood beside her, "Stay here and keep guard over him from a distance." With that, she went home sadly. However, the angel Gabriel was also keeping watch.

God was so angry with Pharaoh and his people that he sent a horrible disease to them, that made them itch and caused great pain. Thermutis, the daughter of Pharaoh, came down to the River Nile to bathe, and to soothe the itch and ache of her sores. As she dipped her arms in the river, she saw the babe adrift in his basket and she knew at once that he was a Hebrew child who should have

drowned. When she heard him cry, she took pity on him and reached out to draw his little ark to shore. As she stretched towards him, all the sores on her arms were healed and her skin became white and soft again. But she could not at first reach the basket because it was too far out. Then as she struggled, her arms lengthened miraculously and she was able to pull the ark to shore.

When she saw such a beautiful child under the covers, she loved him immediately and instructed her maid to feed the hungry baby. But the boy would not feed from her.

All this time Miriam was still watching over the boy from her hiding place. She had not left it for days. When she saw what had happened, she went out fearlessly to the princess and said to her, "O Princess, daughter of Pharaoh, this boy will not take food from anyone but a Hebrew mother. Let me go and find a woman who can feed him."

Thermutis was concerned for the boy and so agreed. "Go! Find such a woman and come directly with her to the palace, for I will take him there and

keep him. I will love and care for him till he grows up." She told her maids to pick up the basket and they returned with it to the palace.

Miriam went home and told her mother all that had happened. Then Jochebed's heart filled with gladness and she ran to the palace to suckle her own child. "Oh, my dearest boy," she murmured as she held him close to her heart, "God has saved you and now I can feed you and watch you grow. Miriam's dream said that you will one day save our people from their slavery, so I will care for you and in secret prepare you for your great work!" Then she laid him in his cradle and he slept peacefully.

Thermutis called this boy Moses, which means "drawn from the waters." Not only did he surpass every other child in beauty, but also in intelligence. Scholars came from all over the world to teach him, but even when he was still a boy, he was wiser than them all. Wherever he went, a light shone round him and his radiance filled the palace.

When he was a man, Moses did save his people, but that is another story!

NOTES

THE MOTHER–SON BOND

The mother–son dyad is biological in origin and it continues to be fraught with strong emotion, which makes it difficult to dissolve. To complicate the issue, many societies have idealized close mother–son relationships. As explored in these tales, problems are intensified by the absence or exclusion of siblings. So often the tales focus on the only son, sometimes the son of a widow, and a poor one at that. Here all the maternal eros is directed at this single boy, thereby endangering his eventual autonomy.

Traditionally fathers were often absent, as in "The Mistress of Fire" where the men are away hunting. In such an environment, sons frequently took the place of the dead/absent partner, caring for their weak or aging mothers. But the tales insist that even in these circumstances, life must press forward and sons must begin their own quests.

When the tales introduce siblings, they are usually dealt with one by one. The eldest goes off first, then the next; the youngest is often the special one, like Snot-Nose, who leaves home last but accomplishes the unexpected. Envy between brothers can derive from competition for the mother's love. Such forces make Kayak ("The Magical Sweetgrass Doll") leave home.

"The Horse and the Sword" is the only story in which the mother dies, but here the boy has a rare stepmother who pushes him into life, protecting him till departure is inevitable and later telling him how to conquer her sister giantesses. All sons who feel "abandoned" by a mother's death (or absence) have to deal with such frightening forces, hopefully by transforming them. In both subtle and crude ways, fairy tales use size as an indicator of psychological prominence.

Moses represents a son's need for authentic maternal care, refusing all but his own mother's milk. And although Pharaoh's daughter, as foster-mother, may satisfy his material needs, she cannot offer that vision of his future that his mother and sister bring.

A particular danger is exemplified by the doting mother, in tales where the son's "preciousness" or beauty are emphasized. "The Changeling of Llanfabon" suggests that the faerie folk are provoked to theft by the devotion of the over-fond mother.

"The Boy and the Seedpod Canoe" shows how potent is the connection between mother and son, in that the cravings of the pregnant mother express her son's own desires. The Maori father has the wisdom to recognize and validate this instinctual interaction between mother and son.

THE MOTHER AND LUCK

In these tales there is an implicit connection between luck, fate and maternal resources. Since the mother is at one time the source of sustenance, she will always carry this energy in some way or another. This is why the son must not be completely severed from the mother's sphere. However, he must learn to trust that the personal mother's resources will be replaced by nourishment that lies beyond her. The world holds enough for the boy who has this confidence; he can take to the road. The perplexing problem is how the mother can give her son sufficient provision for the journey of separation. When she provides food for the road, a sense of abundance is activated and her son will never feel destitute. Hans feels luckier with less and less as he moves nearer his mother's home. He is a "dummling" figure whose wisdom is the wisdom of the gospels. His sense of life, his liberation from material possessions, is deemed foolishness by the world; but clearly his sense of inner resource is rich.

When the mother in a fairy tale is poor, this indicates that she lacks what her child needs. The Nepalese boy in "The Goddess of Luck" refuses his mother's sense of impoverishment. Unwilling to be confined, he sets off, demanding more from life. The Goddess of Luck intervenes in his destiny so that he can keep what he wins. Without a good sense of mother, it is impossible to experience abundance.

SEPARATION

However the mother–son dyad is arranged in these stories, its dissolution is usually implicit. But what son wants to leave when he has all he needs? No wonder some boys see no reason to leave the emotional hearth to initiate development. Snot-Nose is carried away from home by a fierce masculine power that in a paradoxically positive way breaks up the close circle of mother and sons and gives the youth the opportunity to develop his wit. Moses is a victim of patriarchal tyranny, but he is cared for by an authentic mother who accepts danger for her son. When patriarchal or (more positively) paternal force is missing, the boy is handicapped in his separation from his mother. The Maori boy has to go off in search of his father, which separates him physically and emotionally from a generous mother. The potent mother–son dyad must be opened up to larger concerns than the exclusive bond allows. Good mothers invite this enlargement even at their own cost.

THE SON'S JOURNEY

The journey is the chief means by which separation is effected. Some of these tales present boys whose energy is not sufficiently aroused to get out into life. Cinderello actually has to be bribed to leave the hearth; but once he goes, he interacts with the world generously. In "The Horse and the Sword," Sigurd is unwilling to go with his father to the hunt; the fact that there is no intervention by the father suggests that masculine energy is weak.

Kayak is driven to the road by the envy of his brothers. To find and define himself apart from them, he outwits and outperforms them and departs, assisted by his mother. He goes in the shoes she makes for him, then he gives them away to an old man who needs them, marking an expansion of feeling. It is a divine figure in human disguise to whom he gives his mother's gift.

The Nepalese boy's journey is essentially intellectual and spiritual. He encounters gods and goddesses on his path, who support his quest. Very different are the ogre and ogresses Snot-Nose finds in his way, or the giantesses who try to hinder Sigurd.

The Maori son, whose father disappeared before his birth, must go in pursuit of him to make the necessary transition into manhood. He sets out in his seedpod canoe and is committed to the waters with his mother's spell for his safe journey, a vital rite of passage.

HEROES AND MAGIC

Fairy-tale heroes do not fight monsters without the aid of magic. Kayak overcomes the enemy with his sweetgrass doll; Sigurd is assisted by magical gifts stolen by his future bride, Helga, from her father. She mediates the energy needed to survive the onslaught of the giant, just as the wit of the stepmother has preserved him from the giantesses' devouring him. Snot-Nose also overwhelms an ogre and two ogresses by wit rather than by might. Cinderello accomplishes what he must through the service of the blackamoor in his ring, rather than his own natural strength.

Like many traditional heroes, Moses is not reared by his own natural parents, but by a royal foster-mother. But it is the dream of his sister and mother that fosters the boy's destiny as national hero. The Maoris' discovery of the canoe is attributed to the boy who launches himself on the waters in a seedpod, thereby becoming a hero who brings benefits to his people. The boy who is taken into the fire is a different kind of culture hero, passively sacrificed for the survival of the Selkups.

RECURRING SYMBOLS

Rings play an important role in several of the tales. One of the commonest and most ancient symbols of wholeness and values that are timeless, they are hard to acquire and easy to lose. Cinderello's gold ring and the Nepalese boy's ring of diamonds are lost in sea or stream, swallowed by fish and miraculously redeemed when the fish is caught and eaten. The rings come from very special donors and suggest bright new possibilities for self-realization that can easily be lost sight of in the adventures on the road.

Jewels and precious metals usually suggests what we most prize, in nonmaterial terms, and in fairy tales that often has to be given, sacrificed or somehow conjured up out of nowhere. Cinderello, for instance, has to create a road of gold to win his bride. "Hans in Luck" offers a fascinating alternative to this common dynamic. Here an inversion of the alchemist's search is enacted, for rather than turning dross to gold, Hans transforms his lump of gold to a common stone, which he then allows to fall into a well, to be lost in the waters as the rings were lost. But Hans must not redeem his stone. It must stay submerged, perhaps because a whole new set of values must come into being. In "The Goddess of Luck," the common copper coin must be treasured as though it were of equal value to the gold and diamonds the Nepalese boy first acquires.

Water is another recurrent symbol in these tales. Universally, water is the primordial element, the source of life itself, with a vital maternal aspect. It is both destructive and cleansing, fertilizing and rejuvenating, paradoxically giving and destroying life. We see it in flood, initiating Snot-Nose's journey. Water is frozen, accentuating the need for fire in "The Mistress of Fire," where it is also used to assault and destroy fire, its contradictory element. Water is the element in which Moses is placed, preserved from its potentially destructive effect in the little ark. The ark as a symbol is similar to the seedpod canoe discovered by the Maori boy. In Maori culture, the canoe carries a strong sense of the masculine container for the seed, hence a symbol of life itself. Water flows in streams ("The Goddess of Luck") and in wells ("Hans in Luck") and is always needed to quench thirst, physical and spiritual. Indeed, deep flowing water has always carried the sense of the darkest reaches of the psyche, and these are the depths into which the mother–son relationship throw us.

In relation to fire and water, whether the desert or the ice-capped land, and in all encounters with nature, the masculine tendency to master or conquer has to be tempered by a more feminine approach of propitiation to these forces. Mastery and propitiation, the masculine and the feminine, are held in balance in the mature psyche and, on a larger scale, in the healthy civilization.

Most of the tales necessitate an encounter of some kind with the world of animals. Horses, cows, pigs, dogs and red-eyed bitches; snakes; geese, herons, huia birds, pure black hens, cuckoos and cocks; fishes in sea and stream: the whole animal world is presented here, and the attitude adopted by each boy towards these creatures determines whether or not he will succeed in his tasks. Animals are always associated with natural life and with instinct, which must not be overridden in the drive towards manhood. Instinct must not simply be indulged either; the red-eyed bitch must be made to serve Snot-Nose fairly, and so he must be firm with her. Untamed instinct can lead us to a state of inhumanity, represented by the ogre and ogresses.

THE SON'S BRIDE

Few of these tales end with the traditional claiming of the bride. Only three of them show the separating journey's successful completion in the celebration of marriage ("The Magical Sweetgrass Doll," "The Horse and the Sword" and "Cinderello"). For that final step, suggesting the achievement of independence and the capacity for free choice, other sons are still unready, for there is often more to be accomplished when the mother's own needs make final departure difficult. Then attachment to a female partner is delayed. Only when energy is freed from the mother can feeling be transferred to a bride. But the tales at least prepare for that next part of the son's history. One knows that there is another story waiting to begin where the first one ends.

The tales suggest that the son's passage from the first emotional bond with his mother to the final bond with the bride, his maturing beyond the state of a dependent boy to that of man and perhaps father, is most paradoxical. He must leave behind the mother with whom he needs connection, if he is to experience the abundance of life and participate in its regeneration.

AUTONOMY

The complexity of the mother–son relationship is richly demonstrated in these stories, implying the universality of the issues. Both the problems and the solutions for the son lie in the establishment of autonomy, emotional and practical. The boys who are set tasks in these tales are diverse: the Nepalese boy is mentally agile, seeking out the gods to answer deep philosophical questions; Hans and Snot-Nose are dim-witted, the latter being scarcely able to formulate a prayer to God. But wisdom is not a matter of intelligence, these tales suggest, and the deepest wisdom is what all fascinating stories explore and perpetuate. The treasures to be won are independence, confidence and an enlargement of feeling that begins in the mother–son bond but must not be trapped there.

SOURCES

THE GODDESS OF LUCK
Sharma, Man Mohan (ed.), *Folklore of Nepal*, Vision Books, New Delhi, 1978.

THE MAGICAL SWEETGRASS DOLL
Hill, Kay (ed.), *Glooskap and his Magic: Legends of the Wabanaki*, McClelland & Stewart, Toronto, 1983.

SNOT-NOSE
Bjurström, C. G. (ed.), *French Folktales: From the Collection of Henri Pourrat*,
Pantheon Books, New York, 1989.

THE MISTRESS OF FIRE
Riordan, James (ed.), *The Sun Maiden and the Crescent Moon: Siberian Folk Tales*,
Interlink Books, New York, 1989.

THE HORSE AND THE SWORD
Adapted from *Islandische Märchen* in Lang, Andrew (ed.), *The Crimson Fairy Book*,
Dover Publications, New York, 1967.

HANS IN LUCK
Grimm, Jakob and Wilhelm, *Grimms' Fairy Tales*, 1812–15.

THE CHANGELING OF LLANFABON
Jenkyn-Thomas, W. (ed.), *The Welsh Fairy Book*, Unwin, London, 1995.

THE BOY AND THE SEEDPOD CANOE
Orbell, Margaret (tr.), *Maori Folktales in Maori and English*, C. Hurst & Co., London, 1968.
White, John, *The Ancient History of the Maori, His Mythology and Traditions*, vol. 2, Low, Marston,
Searle & Rimington, London, 1889.

CINDERELLO
Megas, Georgiou (ed.), *Folktales of Greece*, Chicago University Press, Chicago, 1970.

MOSES AND THE FAITHFUL MIDWIVES
Ginsberg, Louis, *The Legends of the Jews*, vol. 2, The Jewish Publications Society of America,
Philadelphia, 1909.

3 1161 00694 1366

BAREFOOT BOOKS publishes high-quality picture books for
children of all ages and specializes in the work of artists and writers from
many cultures. If you have enjoyed this book and would like to receive a copy
of our current catalog, please write to our New York office: Barefoot Books,
41 Schermerhorn Street, Suite 145, Brooklyn, New York, NY 11201-4845
email: ussales@barefoot-books.com website: www.barefoot-books.com